Are They Winning?

Susan C. Barto

THIRD EDITION

Library of Congress Control Number:
99-74112

ISBN-10: 0-9712516-3-0
ISBN-13: 9780971251632

Gary Drury's Publishing™

Kentucky

Produced in The United States of America.

DEDICATION

MY BELOVED SON
WILLIAM MICHAEL BARTO, PhD.

CONTENTS

Dedication   5

Finders Keepers,   8

Losers Weepers   8

Footsteps   12

That Damn Float   16

First Date   20

Ice Skating   26

Roller Coaster Ride   31

Are They Winning?   35

Jo Ann's Ring   40

A Profusion Of Lilacs   44

After The Blizzard   48

About The Author   52

Finders Keepers, Losers Weepers

Jill was skipping home from school that beautiful May afternoon when she tripped and went head down toward the grass. Shining in the grass was a spanking new Mickey Mouse watch with a bright red band. Jill felt as though she had been punched with joy. There it was for her to find. She picked it up and fingers trembling with eagerness put it on her wrist.

Now she started to run the rest of the way home singing "Finders Keepers, Losers Weepers" under her breath as she ran. She couldn't wait to show this treasure to her younger brother, John. He was eighteen months younger than she was, but he always seemed wiser to her. She pushed open the front door and shouted for John. Amazingly, he was home before she and came quickly at the sound of her voice.

"Hi, Jill. What's up?"

"John, look what I found:"

"Wow. It looks brand new."

"It was lying in the grass, and I saw it because I fell down. There it was just waiting for me. I know it was meant for me."

For a minute or so they joined hands and cried, "Finders Keepers, Losers Weepers" as they sort of danced in a semi-circle. When their energy was momentarily spent John mused,

"I wonder, though, about the loser. Who lost it, and is the kid sad now?"

"John:" Jill was shocked. "You know that if you find something you get to keep it. Whoever lost it should have been more careful."

"Yeah, you're right. I shouldn't have said anything. I'm sorry. I don't want to spoil things for you."

"It's okay. Only now I wonder whether Mother will let me keep the watch."

"Well, I won't snitch or anything."

"No, I know. I'm going to show and tell her all about it myself as soon as she gets home."

Shortly their Mom did arrive home. She greeted them and headed toward the kitchen to start dinner preparations.

"Mom look what I found on the way home from school."

"Jill, that's gorgeous. What are you going to do with it?"

As far as Jill was concerned, this was turning into a rotten day when just a little while ago everything had been so right. All the gold seemed to go out of the day. That night she was a long time falling asleep. She tortured herself over what John had said. Whoever lost this wonderful watch must be feeling pretty wretched along about now. But still ...The next morning Jill went off to school without saying anything about the watch, and no one in the family not even John asked her about her decision. They all trusted her.

She went directly to Miss Applebee's office and asked to see her. The principal's staff was unused to children's voluntarily coming in to see Miss Applebee, and consequently, ushered Jill in immediately. She, of course, gave the watch to the principal and requested that Miss Applebee try to find the rightful owner.

Jill heard nothing more about the watch for a couple of days, but on the third afternoon when she returned from school John had once again beaten her home. He beamed,

"Jill, look what came for you. A present."

"What? Why? Who is it from?"

"It seems as though your friend Don Snow's little sister, Sue, lost the Mickey Mouse watch. Mrs. Snow called Columbia Grade School, inquired about whether it had possibly been found, and she heard the whole story. Mrs. Snow went right out and bought you this present, and why don't you open it instead of asking questions?"

The present was rectangular and festively gift-wrapped. Jill untied the ribbons and slit open the paper carefully and slowly to make it last longer. Inside she found a large, Disney, pop-up book, CINDERELLA. It had the whole Disney version of the story, and each page popped up pictures - Cinderella in her ball gown, the mice, the coach, the pumpkin, the evil sisters. The pictures were gilt-edged, and the book took Jill's breath away.

The whole family celebrated with Jill that evening at dinner. That night and many nights thereafter before clicking off her light after she had gone to bed, Jill turned the pages of her magnificent book. Of all the Disney movies "Cinderella" had been her favorite. Even though "Beauty and the Beast", "The Lion King" and "The Hunchback of Notre Dame" were newer movies Jill still fancied "Cinderella". Like Cinderella, she had only to wait and work for her happy ending.

Footsteps

Every Wednesday Suzanne escaped from school an hour sooner than most of her classmates. P.S. 215 released the Catholic children early so that they could attend compulsory religious education classes at the Catholic Church. Suzanne considered this a dubious pleasure because the Church was several blocks farther away from home than the school was, and the instruction classes got out so late that she always reached home at dusk or even dark in the winter when it was cold and gloomy. Walking home in the gathering dark when the dim light made objects indistinct until you approached them depressed her. Suzanne wished for a magic carpet to transport her home quickly.

The walk was long, and she often tried going by different routes after she reached the candy store. She never aimed for a route that would bypass the neighborhood store because munching on her store of penny candy would help the weary trek homeward. She always had a couple of pennies with which to choose from the dazzling array of candies available for a penny--licorice in black, chocolate or cherry flavors, wax bottles containing sweet liquid to drink with the wax bottle itself available to chew on when the liquid was gone, little buttons of candy attached to paper, jaw breakers and any manner of assorted sweets.

One afternoon she tried going home by navigating parallel to her own street by walking all the way down 5th Street instead of East 4th Street where she lived. This way ultimately led to her close friend Ellie's house. The friendship between Suzanne and Ellie went back to the first grade when each had been skipped from 1st to 2nd grade and ended up in the same 2nd grade class together. They also had in common the close friendship of Suzanne's cousin Andrea and Ellie's older sister, Janet. Suzanne lived in a two-family house in Brooklyn with Andrea and Andrea's two sisters.

It was particularly raw that winter afternoon and Suzanne was spooked. She became certain that she could hear footsteps behind her, but the twilight made it almost impossible to see clearly. Suzanne was too scared to investigate the footsteps carefully. She just squinted when she peered in back of her. She became positive that the footsteps stopped when she did and resumed when she started back up. Since she was freezing with fear, she decided to try to trick her pursuer. She ducked into a nearby yard and hid behind the garage until she heard the footsteps pass by and felt that she had triumphed. Going forth again she discovered that she was in front of Ellie's house and only a block or so from home and determined to pop in on Ellie. This seemed like a prudent solution to her lingering fear about the footsteps. Unfortunately, her anxiety was also quickened at the same time because while hiding behind the garage she thought she could discern a figure entering what proved now to be Ellie's house. Ellie, herself, opened the door and said,

"Hi. Come on in."

"Ellie, did some sinister figure just come in your house?"

"Sinister figure? Of course not. I don't know what you're talking about. The only person who came in was Andrea to see Janet."

When Suzanne got over her astonishment, she told Ellie about her adventures on the walk home from religious education and her certainty that someone malevolent had been following her.

"It's so gloomy outside that I'm sure Andrea didn't even realize that you were in front of her or she certainly would have called out," Ellie said.

The television was blaring in the den and Howdy Doody was on. In Suzanne's neighborhood nobody would admit to watching Howdy Doody except for Suzanne, and the other children ridiculed her for this. The children claimed to watch Howdy Doody merely for the five minute segment which showed an old time movie.

"I was just watching TV and was about to turn Howdy Doody off because the old time movie just ended," Ellie said.

Suzanne smiled to herself to hear Ellie fib so badly, but she went along with the fiction.

"What do you watch when you turn off Howdy Doody?"

But Ellie finessed and changed the subject to say that Andrea and Janet were up in Janet's room in conference, and she didn't feel that she and Suzanne would be welcome.

"Why are they always so secretive? When we were all

younger we played together. Now we cluster according to age, and it takes away a lot of fun from the neighborhood," Susan said.

"You're so right," Ellie said. "Life was simpler when the groups were larger, and we were smaller."

Suzanne enjoyed being here with Ellie watching Howdy Doody, which Ellie forgot to turn off and knowing that when Andrea came downstairs she could walk the last block or so home in the dark with Andrea by her side. Good smells of dinner cooking wafted from the kitchen.

The best part of arriving home after dark was that when she and Andy sighted their house the bright yellow light glowed from behind the curtains, blinds and shades and welcomed them to family and dinner. Each bad event like the long, frigid walk from religious education has its compensations Suzanne thought.

That Damn Float

Pete pinned Maryann, and he picked her up every day after school. Susan and Maryann were in high school in their Junior year. From the seventh period projection crew room where the girls reigned as they were the only girls on the projection crew, they spied his car from the window. Susan envied the free time Pete seemed to have; for Harry, his fraternity brother and her love, was extremely serious about studying, and he spent all his spare time doing it as well as working at a part-time job. Since Maryann and Pete were going steady, and Susan and Harry had such an agreeable relationship, the subject of their also going steady cropped up prematurely as it turned out. The first summer of their relationship after a two-week stint at National Guard camp Harry asked Susan to wear his fraternity pin. She was thrilled. Being pinned was far more adult than wearing a boy's school ring on a chain around your neck. Her family was not pleased as she was expected to go to college for four years and still had two more years of high school.

Finally the memorable day of their pinning arrived, and that Wednesday afternoon Harry was spotted along with Pete from the projection crew room window. The four of them fashioned a ceremony around Harry's pinning Susan, and the two couples were officially a foursome. As soon as Susan had Harry's pin things began to change. For one thing Harry had just been elected to an office in his fraternity, Alpha Phi Omega, and this anointed him with status in the eyes of the fraternity's sister sorority, Phi Omega Chi. The sorority sisters felt enraged that both Pete and Harry were dating high school girls instead of dating them. Susan always blamed homecoming weekend and "that damn float" for their unpinning. Harry's fraternity was building a float for the homecoming parade preceding the football game, and subsequently many evenings were spent at this activity, and Susan and Maryann joined in painting the float with everyone else to the chagrin of the sorority sisters. One evening prior to painting the float Susan had dinner at Harry's house and was naturally dressed in her best for the occasion wearing a new beige London Fog trench coat that made her look like Mata Hari, and even better than that was the most slenderizing garment she had ever owned. That night while painting the float she got a splotch of royal blue poster paint on the new trench coat, and it never seemed as good again. The float depicted "An American In Paris" - the theme that homecoming year was Academy Award winning movies, and it wound up winning second place although it deserved first place because "The Bridge on the River Kwi` float which did win the blue ribbon was so topical, the movie's recently having won the Academy Award. From that evening on the splotch of paint began to seem like an omen, and Susan subsequently referred to the float as

17

"that damn float", and she resented it before she really knew why.

Homecoming weekend began on Friday afternoon when Harry picked her and Maryann up and took them to Peter's house where both girls spent the night. Peter's mother made traditional Friday night macaroni and cheese with an added special surprise of tomato sauce, and after eating the four went out to the college campus where fraternity brothers and sorority sisters were putting final touches to the float. The night was unseasonably cold for October, and Susan and Maryann spent most of the evening in Pete's car with the heater on trying to keep from freezing and cursing the float. The Phi Omegas were delighted by their defection, and eventually the boys drove them to Pete's house to sleep while they stayed out all night working with the sorority sisters on the float. This turn of events infuriated Susan.

The homecoming parade with the float contest and the football game that followed were all right, and the girls went back to Pete's house to change for the dinner dance. The dance was uneventful except that Harry seemed so preoccupied, which she chalked up to his being tired and grumpy from staying up all night. When at the fraternity dinner before the dance the boys were asked to introduce themselves and their girls, Harry said,

"My name is Harry, and this is my date, Sue."

"Date," she heard a fraternity brother say. "She's wearing his pin."

Susan's sentiments exactly, and she looked so pretty that night too in her new evening gown, black with that new bubble skirt. Susan knew then that something was amiss, and she didn't have long to wait to find out what. The following Friday Harry was slotted to pick her up where she was ushering at the Drama Club's evening play, and he came as planned. They went for a ride, and Harry announced somewhat sheepishly that he didn't want to be pinned any longer, although he claimed to care still about Susan and wanted things to continue as usual except that they both could date other people.

Susan was in a quandary. She received advice from all her friends which ranged from "Drop him" and "Call that friend Ray of his and go to the next event with him. He seems to have a crush on you." Nothing made too much sense until she talked with her friend Betty who said,

"If you love him, just hang in there and do nothing. Things will work out."

Betty proved to be right, for Harry's wild dating binge ended up as only two dates, neither of which he seemed to enjoy so far as Susan could infer. Between Betty's being so supportive - she approved of Susan and Harry as she thought they fit together so well when they hugged - the attentions of a boy who had given up on her while she was pinned, and Harry's treating her as romantically as ever and actually spending as much time with her as ever, Susan got through this patch. Harry made sure that they were together on New Year's Eve saying that he could never spend it with anyone else since they had met on a New Year's Eve blind date. Although they didn't get repinned, within a year they were engaged.

As for "that damn float" — it had only won second prize, torn a rift in Susan and Harry's relationship, and would permanently remain a thorn in Susan's paw. Homecoming was never again to be her favorite weekend, but Spring weekend held aloft the promise of orange blossoms.

First Date

Elizabeth first noticed Jim during the flurry of the pre-Christmas season. Certainly, she later remembered asking Betty to invite him to her Caroling party as her date. She also asked Betty to invite Skip in case Jim couldn't make it. This precaution proved to be prudent because Jim skipped the Caroling party for some reason, and Elizabeth missed seeing Jim until the evening of the Christmas Cotillion at Canoe Brook Country Club held the night before Christmas Eve. This Cotillion was a biannual event in conjunction with the ballroom dancing group which Elizabeth and all her set attended weekly throughout the year. By the time they were juniors and seniors the dancing classes had become dances and the young people could attend with dates if they preferred or stag if they so chose. Elizabeth, however, being only twelve and in the seventh grade in Junior High still thought of the events as dancing class. The Christmas Cotillion included a formal dinner at the Country Club prior to the main event, and the chaperones in charge assigned the boys and girls to dinner partners. Elizabeth felt lucky to be seated with Bob, a boy she had earlier that year had a crush on. His desires lay elsewhere so she didn't expect his exclusive attentions during the dance.

The dance itself proved to be dreamlike, and she found herself dancing with Jim. How the partnership evolved she didn't recall but they stayed coupled for the entire dance to Elizabeth's delight. Jim didn't act shy with her, and the two engaged in banter and good humored flirtation. There was a scary mix-up after the dance. Elizabeth had attended a party before the formal dinner, and the chaperones had seen to the transportation of the whole group. Thinking that Elizabeth had thus obtained a ride home as well, her father neglected to pick her up. The night air was frigid, and after twenty minutes of standing in the cold waiting for her father, Elizabeth wandered inside and telephoned home. Within minutes her father arrived apologizing throughout the ride home for the mix-up. However, since Elizabeth floated as if being carried up in a balloon from the effects of the dance, even the misadventure of her almost missed ride couldn't diminish her pleasure in the evening.

Since the next day brought Christmas Eve and then the holiday itself, family things took precedence. Christmas week vacation included a trip to New York City with her girlfriends, and the week ended with a baby sitting job on New Year's Eve, which was sweetened by sharing the job with her close friend Betty. Also the child for whom they were sitting was only a couple of grades behind them in school, but she was afraid to be left at home alone so the three girls had a New Year's Eve Party. At midnight they telephoned friends to wish them a Happy New Year. Feeling energized by the occasion, Elizabeth and Betty called Jim as well as Betty's boy of the moment.

"Elizabeth, what a surprise. I was just telephoning you. Can you go to see "White Christmas" with me at the Strand on Saturday evening our last weekend before school starts?"

"Jim, I'd love to. I'll see you then."

What a delightful twist this brought to the girls' festivities, and how happy Betty was for her.

This date was to be Elizabeth's official first date. She had been to co-ed movie parties and house parties, but this date would be her first alone with a boy. Unfortunately, Jim's parents would chauffeur them to and from the movie, but as this was the only transportation method available to dating Junior Highs, Elizabeth accepted this situation. She sat hushed and expectant in the movie theatre while the film began. It was an opulent, color musical, a remake of the old "Holiday Inn", and had lavish sets, music and dancing, and it was their last chance to enjoy Christmas along with the movie which was about Christmas. After the two sat quietly in their seats for about a half hour, Jim put his arm first around the back of the seat and gradually around Elizabeth. This was a thrilling sensation for Elizabeth, and she froze in place while his arm was around her shoulder.

After the movie Jim's parents agreed to let Jim spend an hour or so at Elizabeth's, as her father had promised to drive him home before his deadline. Jim and Elizabeth went to the TV room where Elizabeth's mom served hot chocolate and cookies. Even Elizabeth's parents approved of Jim, which made the evening that much more agreeable.

The big test occurred the following Monday back at school. Elizabeth suspected that Jim was absent from school early on as she didn't spot him at any of their usual haunts. Her hunch proved to be correct, but he appeared in the hall the following day. He seemed hesitant and much more shy than he had ever seemed before, and he indicated to her that some of his fellow Hi-Y members of the Vikings had ribbed him about their date. Girls, Elizabeth ruminated, never minded their friends' knowing about their love lives, and she wondered why boys were so troubled by the teasing. Elizabeth and Jim continued to see each other at the weekly ballroom dancing, and Elizabeth felt satisfied because Jim always managed to dance with her more than with anyone else.

In the meantime Elizabeth and her friends were planning a couples only Valentine's party at Elizabeth's house. Of course, Elizabeth was inviting Jim to be her date, and Betty who was involved with a boy named Daniel was planning to invite him. The preparations were numerous and involved the buying of many sacks of red fiery cinnamon hearts to put in a jar for a guess the number of cinnamon hearts contest. Betty and Elizabeth counted the blasted candies as they plopped them into the jar, and the contest would be among the remainder of the guests to approximate the number for a prize. Elizabeth's parents complained that due to the jar's overturning during the festivities, and everyone's grabbing handfuls to eat they found red hearts on the rug and hiding all around the living room and TV room for several years thereafter. The girls purchased new outfits, sent out the coveted invitations specifying that each girl was to bring a date, and eventually the day of the Valentine's party arrived.

Fortunately, Jim arrived as Elizabeth's trophy date and the major reason for the party's happening. The party took off as promptly as a spaceship launch and stayed in orbit. Climaxing the evening was a game of Spin the Bottle, during which all the players involved cheated securing the desired effect of the couples pairing off together with an excuse to kiss. For the last spin of the bottle a contest ensued allowing all the couples to kiss with the spin, and a prize to go to the couple who held the kiss the longest. Betty and Daniel engaged in quite the showiest kiss feigning urgent passion whereas Jim and Elizabeth simply enjoyed a romantic kiss which certainly lasted the longest. However, Betty's dramatic kiss won the prize, and the party was over.

Back at school Elizabeth and Jim's relationship slowed down temporarily for a short while until both of them got involved in the political campaign of a mutual friend for school president, and both were invited to take part in a campaign skit to be held in the auditorium on campaign day, the day before school elections. Elizabeth loved this interval. She and Jim met at skit rehearsals every afternoon, and Jim walked her home although it was really out of his way. By the time the skit was staged in front of the audience they were joined together as a couple again. Sure enough, the following week, Jim invited Elizabeth to go to the movies to see "On the Waterfront" and "A Member of the Wedding." The choice of movies seemed fortuitous, as both were thought provoking movies and gave rise to much discussion both quiet and heated between the two. Once again, Jim put his arm around Elizabeth, and he even held her hand for a while, which was strangely more intimate. The two movies proved emotionally draining, but Elizabeth felt on the same intellectual wave length as Jim, and the evening ended satisfactorily.

A mystery! Back at school the following week Jim turned cool. He continued to be friendly, but something seemed to be out of whack. However, there were no rumors circulating about a break up or Jim's caring about another girl so Elizabeth chalked it up to joking at Jim's expense done by the Vikings. For a short while things remained static. Jim danced with Elizabeth at the dances, but made no further advances towards her. During this impasse between her and Jim, Elizabeth developed a serious crush on Chuck, one of the most popular boys in the Junior High and a fellow Viking with Jim.

Chuck and she clicked at the dances, with Chuck's dancing a good part of the evenings with her. Things came to a boil when Jim decided to give a couples only party for the Vikings. Elizabeth, who was dizzy with the force of her feelings for Chuck, prayed and even wished on a star for Chuck to ask her to Jim's party, though deep down she felt this was a hopeless desire. One night while doing her homework she wished on the first star which she could see from her desk, and the phone rang bringing the desired invitation to Jim's Viking party.

The phone call was the beginning of Elizabeth and Chuck's special relationship. Shortly after the news about the party leaked out a rumor circulated that Jim had suggested to Chuck that he ask Elizabeth, his apparently having observed them at the dance. Elizabeth never minded this rumor. She felt pleased that if it should happen to be true that Jim had gone to this trouble on her behalf. He obviously didn't want to see her hurt. Then, too, if it were true then her first date had led to this unique and precious interlude with Chuck, who if he hadn't been her first date had been her first serious affair of the heart.

Ice Skating

Meg's crowd ice skated before Lynn moved to town. When they all attended grade school ice skating was a part of life in the winter. The town they lived in froze the tennis courts at Memorial Field each winter, and the first frosty day news of the tennis courts' freezing would float through the school. Shouts of joy rang out, and the children ran home and changed into skating clothes then grabbed their skates and greeted each other at the frozen tennis courts. When it became cold enough Meg spent entire Saturday mornings at the tennis courts skating with her friends until her cheeks were rosy and her feet numb. Saturday afternoons were usually reserved for the movies. When they grew a little older the young people held skating parties which were most often coed. Liz had a unique skating party because she provided transportation to a nearby lake with smooth skating ice. Meg remembered that she bought a real short ice skating skirt made of black velvet and lined with cherry red satin for Liz's party and enjoyed skating with Tony who noticed the skirt. Lynn moved to town when they were sophomores in high school. Before her arrival ice skating wasn't as vital to their lives as it had been formerly. However, Lynn discovered a frozen pond across town which boasted smooth ice, a bonfire to help keep them from freezing and available hot chocolate. Lynn's approval meant a lot to Meg's crowd at this time since Lynn had much clout and influence for a new girl. Although not conventionally pretty, she was spirited and intelligent, and her flirtatious ways attracted many of the boys in Meg's crowd. The girls too drew into her circle, and before Meg quite knew how it had happened, Lynn was a member of her group. It was a coup of sorts for Meg's crowd which hovered near the top of the groups but usually took second place in prestige. Lynn's entrance in the group pushed the group up a notch. Lynn possessed natural leadership qualities, and her attentions were sought after.

Lynn dated many boys in the top crowd, but after a few months she settled upon John. John was a gorgeous looking boy who was popular and possessed a terrific sense of humor. She and John were a couple at the time Lynn gave her first important party. Meg felt glad to be invited and spent the elephant's share of her clothes allowance on a designer dress. It was a dinner or theatre dress with a jacket in a white silky material trimmed in a luscious shade of pink. Meg was not attached to any one boy at the time of the party and looked upon the event as a possible hunting ground where she might meet her newest boyfriend. She did end up with a new boyfriend after the party, but the circumstances surrounding this happening were unexpected and surprised Meg. Shortly after the party began Meg noticed John's paying a lot of attention to her. Lynn was her usual animated and vivacious self, so Meg took a little time before realizing that something was amiss between Lynn and John. As the party progressed Meg basked in John's obvious interest in her. John divided his time between dancing each dance with Meg and staying by her side the rest of the time. Meg was flustered but pleased. Meg began to worry whether Lynn might hold a grudge against her for stealing so much of John's time at the party, but Lynn was as cordial as ever when Meg left the party. Lynn as always had not lacked admiration from the rest of the boys at the party, and if she were suffering, she was certainly concealing it well.

A few days after Lynn's party John telephoned Meg and asked her to go to the movies with him on the weekend. Meg was startled as she had figured that maybe John was just trying to pull Lynn's strings at the party and that by now they'd be back together. When she realized that he was serious she accepted his invitation. This left her with the problem of what Lynn would say or do when she heard about this. She decided to confront the problem directly and picked up the phone and called Lynn.

"Meg, of course I don't mind. John and I are split. Go, you'll have fun."

If she were hurt she wasn't showing it, and Meg knew that Lynn wouldn't be sitting home alone on Saturday night. John looked a little shy, handsome as ever, and much less like the class clown when he picked Meg up for their date. Meg had a new dress on and was a little nervous. They walked the few blocks to the movie theatre. Although it was winter, the air was mild for the season. During the movie John behaved like a perfect date putting his arm around the back of the chair and only towards the end of the film touching Meg's shoulder.

He asked whether Meg wanted to walk home through the park which although longer was a more scenic route than the one they traversed on the way to the movies. Meg warily agreed afraid that John might get fresh once they were alone in the park. However, nothing untoward happened, and before she knew it they were back at the house with Meg's mother making an offer of cocoa. They were in the television room when Meg's mother said,

"I'll be right back with some cocoa and cookies."

To Meg's astonishment the moment her mother was out of sight John reached for her with what appeared to be six hands and started to kiss and grope. Amazed, Meg commenced to field the passes and grab his hands, and her mother was back with the cocoa before any trouble could escalate. John seemed self-possessed and unfazed by the proceeding events and Meg's halting actions. The evening ended on a cheerful and calm note, and John went off on his way. Meg shared a bit of the evening's events with her mother who was always willing to commiserate, and Meg said,

"Boys never cease to amaze me. You just never know what they are going to do next."

Meg felt in the dark about what to do next. By midweek the scenerio became a bit clearer. Meg's best friend, Jean, said in passing,

"If you want to keep John as a boyfriend, you better start going skating."

The hint had portent and innuendo for Meg. She realized that Jean was talking about skating at the place Lynn discovered and haunted. Simultaneously, she surmised that John and Lynn were skating together and presumably sharing cups of hot chocolate. Telling herself that she wanted to go skating anyway, Meg went to the frozen pond. Sure enough, John and Lynn were back together skating and alternately sitting on the benches around the pond warming up. Meg figured it all out while she skated around the pond. Probably, Lynn and John argued or had some kind of tiff just prior to Lynn's party. It must have been around that time or John wouldn't have been invited to the party. John must have punished Lynn by flirting with Meg and trying to make her jealous. Obviously, the ploy worked since here they were together, and Meg was frozen out.

Meg decided to be pragmatic instead of bitter. After all no harm had been done; it was just a date and an odd one at that. The experience had been revealing; she now knew more about John than she had before. She wondered, however, whether Lynn allowed those kind of advances or whether he had saved this ploy for her and other girls who were not Lynn. She never found out. The ice skating that evening was not wasted since Tony was there. She hadn't seen or dated him in a while, and that evening they re-newed their friendship and began dating again. As for John, he wrote the following in her yearbook when they were all graduating,

"Do you remember our date in sophomore year?"

Roller Coaster Ride

Dates with Jim flustered Samantha at all times, but tonight they were going to Olympic Park, their area's answer to Atlantic City before the casinos. Tonight's date might turn out to be thrilling. He showed up on Samantha's doorstep half-an-hour late as usual. Samantha knew this was because he calculated that Samantha would be half-an-hour late each time. The timing was perfect. Jim was two years older than Samantha and a Junior to her Sophomore. He boast an aura of self-confidence which accentuated his tall almost massive frame. Jim was Samantha's interesting older man of the moment. Sam had never been to Olympic Park before and was clueless regarding its attractions.

The summer night was balmy, and the car windows were open wide letting the breezes waft in. When they got to Olympic Park Jim shot at every duck, gambled on every wheel, and pitched at every milk bottle to try to win Samantha a prize. Luck touched them at a coin toss where the prize was a putrid green, stuffed frog, which Samantha revered simply because Jim had triumphed to win it. They wandered along, holding hands and alternating between playing the games of chance and eating frozen custards. Jim said,

"If you want cotton candy, we should have it after the rides in case we start to feel queasy."

The whip came first, and Samantha loved it as she had loved it since childhood. They snuggled together until the whip lurched sending them apart and then back together. When Jim suggested the Ferris Wheel Sam demurred because it looked terrifying to be up so high. However, the Ferris Wheel turned out to be romantic. The pace of the ride was dreamy, and it didn't jar them enough to be scary. The wheel stopped when their car was on top, and Samantha and Jim contemplated the stars which seemed to be so close from that vantage point.

The fear started when they got down from the Ferris Wheel and Jim mentioned the Roller Coaster.

"The Roller Coaster: I've never been on one in my life. I don't think so."

"Samantha, you'll hate yourself if we don't ride it before we go home. We'll feel like we failed."

Samantha knew what Jim meant. She could never leave the community pool unless she had jumped from the high dive no matter how frightened she was. Sometimes she even made herself dive from it.

"Why not. We only live once," she finally agreed.

Once on line to buy tickets for the Roller Coaster, Samantha felt as trapped as she did on the diving board. To turn back now would be unthinkable like descending the steps down from the diving board's heights instead of leaping or diving into the water. It was worse than getting in the dentist's chair - that was only painful, this could be fatal.

Nothing could have prepared Samantha for the actuality of the ride. The cars started to climb, and she thanked God that theirs wasn't the first car. Dipping down with no other car in front would have been more horrible than the experience already was. The first small dip felt like plunging down a mountain without skis, but they survived. Suddenly the car was climbing up so straight a path that it seemed as though the descent would be a 90 degree angle one with nowhere else for them to go except out into space.

We can't be going up this high she thought. We'll plummet out from the car. This bar isn't that secure. For that matter how sturdy were the tracks and the rattling, rickety cars? As they started the fearsome drop Samantha heard herself scream,

"Jim, if we get out of here alive I'll love you forever."

She recalled screaming and squealing like every cliche told about people on Roller Coasters. Her black hair whipped and flailed around her shoulders, and her brown eyes were feverish. Jim remained as steady as a boulder, and Samantha's finger nails were digging into his hand. She clutched on to him frantically. She dreaded each up, and agonized each down. Finally the ride was over. Every muscle quivering, Samantha exited the car.

"Not so fast, Sam. I remember what you said about loving me forever if we survived this. We're going up again."

Adamant, Jim purchased two more tickets and prodded Sam back into the car. The second ride shook Samantha to her roots as much as the first ride. The heights and depths scared Samantha as much as before. However, when the seemingly endless ride ended, Samantha had been through a trial by motion. She wobbled off the car and teetered away from the Roller Coaster. She felt purged and reborn.

"Jim, it was fabulous. Almost a supernatural experience. I could get hooked on this."

The evening continued as though enchanted. They gobbled cotton candy after the ride sitting on a bench and sharing sticky sweet kisses. They preened over their bravery and exchanged tales about men they knew who were afraid to ride the Roller Coaster.

Their relationship itself bobbed up and down like the Roller Coaster ride. They broke up and reunited often both before this date at Olympic Park and after it. The Roller Coaster ride climaxed their connection. Samantha became a Roller Coaster freak, riding each one she came upon. She experienced many evenings at Olympic Park with different dates, and always the place held magic. No ride ever equaled that first one, but all were memorable.

Are They Winning?

Walking down the residential streets of Brooklyn on soft summer afternoons, Susan heard the sounds of radios, and the televisions that belonged to the lucky handfuls, blaring out the ball game.

"Are they winning?" she'd ask at regular intervals of people she knew and a few she didn't know.

To almost everyone who lived in Brooklyn in the late 1940's and 1950's 'they' referred to the inimitable Brooklyn Dodgers.

"Who? Them bums: Why don't you ripen your tastes and root for the Yankees like your brother and I do. The Yankees appeal to more mature palettes," Susan's father, who grew up in Manhattan, would tease mercilessly.

Her father's being a Yankee fan frustrated Susan, but she was even more irked by her brother, Bill's, preference for those 'Damn Yankees'. Yankee fans living on the streets of Brooklyn were an affront to the entire neighborhood. Susan's best friend, Bubbles, also had an aberration

- she rooted for the Giants, the Dodger's formidable foe in the National league. This annoyed Susan slightly less because at least the Giants posed a different sort of threat to her beloved Dodgers, and they were in the same league. Also Bubbles had some strange reason for cheering on the Giants; Susan thought perhaps Bubbles' father might be similarly misguided.

Baseball formed an integral part of the fabric of the Borough of Brooklyn. It was something the entire borough had in common - an avid, fanatical worship of the Brooklyn Dodgers. In fact, Susan mused didn't fanatical refer back to the word fan?

For all that her father professed to dislike the Dodgers, he was right there through most of the summer watching them on television playing ball. When he splurged for tickets to ball games for him and Bill, Susan's father always went to a Yankee game, but at home like the rest of Brooklyn the family watched the Dodgers. Susan harbored a grudge for all of her life that it never occurred to her father to buy tickets for at least one Dodger game and take her as well as her brother. Susan's father's rooting, whether for the Yankees or for the Dodgers, was noisy to the ultimate degree. He was loud when he watched the Yankees and rooted vociferously, but when he watched the Dodgers his sounds were deafening because he alternated cheering with hurling insults at the Dodgers like a fan in the stands might propel bottles on the playing field.

Susan and her father were in a heated debate about the merits of the Yankees vs. the Dodgers all summer long, but this warfare escalated to a crescendo during the play-offs and the World Series. Both play-offs during the glory time in the fifties were usually successful for Susan, Bill, and their father as the Yankees usually squared off against the Dodgers in the end. But, oh the rivalry in the days of the Series!

Every year during the Series Susan and her father had a five dollar bet going. Her father loved the Series so much that each year he took a day off from work (or called in sick) to go to Yankee stadium to see one of the games. This was before all the Series games were held at night, so everyone carried portable radios to school and the work place. Teachers in Brooklyn even allowed the radios in the classrooms to catch the score while the World Series was going on if the Yankees and the Dodgers were at it again, and they usually were.

Each year the Yankees won the series and each year Susan owed her father $5.00. It was, however, easy for her to welsh on the bet since he never seriously expected to receive it nor would he have taken it from her. Each October would end with Susan's cry of,

"Wait till next year:"

History, in general, wasn't Susan's favorite subject, but even she knew some baseball history. She read somewhere that the name Dodgers referred to dodging trolleys and that the Dodgers were born in 1883 although they didn't settle on their current name until 1932. Brooklyn baseball fans had their own vocabulary - everyone no matter how young knew what seventh inning stretch referred to. The children collected baseball cards, although the boys traded them more frequently than the girls who preferred trading cards at that time. Everyone chewed TOPS bubble gum that came with the cards. All this baseball mania was part of what one newspaper article called "Dodgerness". Susan revered the players. Duke Snyder, Gil Hodges, Jackie Robinson, and Roy Campanella were like friends she had never met.

37

When Susan was twelve years old her family moved to the suburbs of New Jersey, but the move didn't diminish her love for the Dodgers. Finally one October afternoon in the fifties the Dodgers beat the Yankees while Susan was sitting in the bleachers watching a high school football game which had been postponed from the previous Saturday because the original game washed away because of rain. Betty, Liz and the rest of her friends were cheering wildly for their football team, but Susan wished that the entire stadium would shut up and allow her to listen to the baseball game on the radio, which seemed to be cemented to her ear. After all these years of praying for the Dodgers to trounce the Yankees and win the World Championship, it looked as if it were going to happen without her cheers, without her watching, even without her being able to hear (except in quiet spots) who was winning. A nasty, raw drizzle was supplementing Susan's misery. The injustice of not being able to savor what seemed to be the victory she had prayed for all of her life, but instead to be stuck here in the rain pretending to give a darn about what was happening on the field, and even worse watching the soggy cheerleaders giving dispirited cheers with luke-warm responses from the bleachers. No one seemed to share or even understand why Susan was attached to that portable radio nor why she abruptly leaped to her feet and commenced screaming incoherently that the Dodgers were at last the World Champions. Since her team was far from winning on the football field at the time she lunged screaming to her feet, her behavior was considered un-called for.

However, when she finally returned home not even knowing whether the football team had won or not (the game was tied when the Dodgers cinched their title) her

38

father was waiting for her smiling and holding aloft the coveted $5 bill. Suddenly, it didn't seem to matter that she was cold and damp and that she had missed relishing the triumph which had so long been denied to her. Her father and her brother, Bill, while they didn't share her emotions, certainly didn't begrudge her the joy that was so obviously washing over her.

"So, Susan, them bums finally beat the Yankees! Well, what do you know?"

For that year at least, the Dodgers were the best baseball team in the world. It was time for her father and Bill to shout,

"Wait till next year!"

Jo Ann's Ring

Jo Ann's bravado overwhelmed me the first time I met her. We were seventh graders, and superficial things mattered; but Jo Ann's chubby figure, teeth in need of braces, and too adult permed hair receded into the background under the force of her personality. She was brash, almost abrasive, and super intelligent. In charge of her own persona, she exuded confidence. She didn't seem to envy her peers, although many displayed beauty with superb figures to go along with the faces and marvelous hair.

Most of us were just discovering boys and testing the dating waters with co-ed parties and tentative occasional dates. Jo Ann ripped our social mores to shreds with her comments about the other classmates of both sexes. She felt as comfortable mocking boys as girls, and although her remarks were often cruel they often managed to hone in on the truth. I forget how our acquaintance ripened into friendship. I thought about her with a mix of pity and awe, with the awe mostly winning over the pity. She had a difficult home life as her parents engaged in emotional war, but she said little about this. Many of us had difficult times at home, but we managed to have a life in school apart from the turmoil at home. Indeed we thought of the life with our friends and in school as our real life, certainly the important one. Here is where Jo Ann stood out because her real life at school was almost at a standstill. She and I enjoyed each other's company, but she didn't mingle with many of the others. The force of her personality convinced most of the group that she was above mixing with them.

The minus points in my friendship with Jo Ann included her frankness with me. Although I found it refreshing, I also felt insulted by it much of the time. I tried to dismiss the less than flattering remarks by putting them down to jealousy for as far as I knew she had never had a date. However, she excelled at using put-downs with such authority that I always wondered whether she were right about me.

The Spring of our eighth grade year bustled with parties, dates, and plans for social events. I oozed happiness because I was dating a popular boy I just adored. Riding high, I paid little attention to Jo Ann at this juncture. One morning she turned up at school with a boy's prep school ring on a chain around her neck. The school buzzed with talk about this amazing event. Who was he? Where had she met him? Why hadn't any of us ever heard about him? My other friends dispatched me to find out all about Jo Ann's ring. After all, I was the closest to her.

"Jo Ann give about the ring. Who is he?"

"You remember my telling you about my friend Janet who lives in Lincoln. I've also talked about her brother Bob. He and I are going steady."

She had mentioned them but only in the context of their family's being close with hers. They lived about an hour's drive away, and I'd never met either of them. Jo Ann clearly enjoyed our surprise, and the gossip that surrounded her. She loved being the center of all of it. The mystery enveloping her deepened. She impressed us as she had intended to do. Every time I questioned her about Bob or hinted about meeting him or double dating with them, she reminded me about the distance. Since none of us nor our dates could drive, it was a valid reason for any plans to be dropped. Summer came and with it the close of school. Since she and I were at that point school friends only, I didn't see her again until school started. I privately doubted her relationship with Bob, but I never expressed my skepticism to her. Even if I had known for sure that she'd fabricated the whole episode, I would have kept silent in front of her and all my friends. I felt it was a point of honor.

When school started again in September of ninth grade, Jo Ann arrived transformed. She had undergone a metamorphosis and evolved into a butterfly with smooth hair, a slim figure, and attractive face. Even her teeth were in the process of becoming straightened. Always confident, now she shone with self assurance. Now she attracted friends male and female like electricity. She fit in with the false standards of our school and age group.

To me, however, her new self only reflected outwardly what she had always projected by her enigmatic smile and her flip ways. She'd always inspired respect in me. Her whole evolution began with the incident of the ring. Perhaps the attention the ring evoked helped spur her whole self on to action. For surely if she'd had any baby fat or baby's lack of experience, they were gone now. When she finally told me that the ring had been a prank it was my turn to be inscrutable. She never learned that I held any suspicions about Bob. Our friendship blossomed because for once I could keep still.

A Profusion Of Lilacs

When the Lyric family entered into the lives of Claire Ellen's family a song entered with them. Claire Ellen's family moved to New Providence before the Easter break of Eric's second grade year. Claire Ellen saw that so far Eric's unhappiness over the move was affecting the entire family. She knew Eric wanted to meet friends, but the closest children in the neighborhood who lived in a house whose backyard touched theirs were older and bullies besides. Claire Ellen watched Eric make friendly overtures to them, but evidently, the boys enjoyed teasing him relentlessly while appropriating his toys the few times they pretended to be friendly.

Right before school started again after the break, a boy around Eric's age appeared on the lawn as Claire Ellen and Eric were sitting on the patio.

"Hi," he said shyly, his eyes on the ground. "I understand that we both have the same second grade teacher, Mrs. Anthony. I'm Glen."

With these words a friendship began. Claire Ellen,

delighted that the boys got along beautifully, began to learn a little bit about Glen. He said that he had four brothers ranging in age from six to fourteen. What a handsome crew they turned out to be. Claire Ellen discovered that Eric's friendship with Glen included friendship with all the Lyric boys. Now the bullies fled before the combined strength of the Lyric brothers. Eric had champions. Claire Ellen,, thrilled for Eric found a bonus of her own. She visited Glen's mother, and soon she and Lois Lyric embarked on an enduring closeness of their own. The two women bonded instantly.

Eric's only child status caused Claire Ellen to encourage his friends to play in her house and yard. She lavished attention on the boys when they seemed to want it, and tactfully left them to their own devices when they preferred to be alone. The Lyric boys seemed pleased that Claire Ellen and their mother enjoyed each others company so much. Lois got Claire Ellen involved repairing books at the school library. On the first day that Claire Ellen started repairing books, she was told by another mother who was also working there that day that Glen was looking forward to her arrival.

"Glen?" Claire Ellen asked. "Don't you mean Eric?"

"No, Glen. He told me all about your coming. I think he has a little crush on you."

Claire Ellen compiled all the clues, Glen's pleasure in her friendship with his own mother, his never looking her directly in her eyes, and she felt flattered. What a compliment this was. She determined to handle it gently and watch it flicker to a natural dimming.

A few days later Claire Ellen answered the doorbell and found Glen standing there holding a profusion of lilacs. The aroma perfumed the air, and Claire Ellen thought they were awesome like Glen and his brothers.

"Thank you, Glen. There are no flowers in my garden as beautiful as these. I never saw such spectacular lilacs, and the scent is filling the room. Let's get them in a vase." Later when Claire Ellen mentioned the lilacs to Lois, thinking that perhaps they had been her idea, Lois claimed no knowledge of them whatsoever. She seemed surprised and amused. Claire Ellen knew she should tread gently with this crush of Glen's as she had learned only the other day how sensitive he was. She and Lois had been lounging on Lois's patio and the three Lyric brothers closest to Eric's age were playing in the backyard when Glen rushed inside in tears. Lois excused herself to go in to him, and when she came out she amazed Claire Ellen by saying,

"Glen worries that Scott and Dean are taking over his friendship with Eric. He, after all, was the one who met Eric first, and they are the original buddies. Scott and Dean since they are less shy often overwhelm Glen and try to take over his friends."

Claire Ellen absorbed this and realized that it should have been obvious to her, and as soon as possible she shared the new found information with Eric hoping that he could help rectify it. Eric, empathic as always, resolved to try to fix the situation without Glen's realizing that he knew how upset Glen had been and why.

Once school was out the boys fished and swam the summer away. Lois and Claire Ellen joined the community pool, and all of them went each day from before lunch time until dinner. Claire Ellen and Lois relished this time. observing the boys enjoying the air and water and sharing the responsibility of watching them with the life guards seemed like a slice of perfection. The life guards benched the young swimmers without ever reporting to the parents.

Eric and the Lyric boys ran a carnival for Jerry's kids that same summer, and the two families, husbands included, went to New York City to the telethon, and the boys gave the money to Jerry Lewis.

By September Claire Ellen noticed that Eric's attempts to convince Glen of the strength of their friendship had succeeded, and the trust between them seemed to grow each month. As for Claire Ellen's worries about handling the crush, Glen discovered the girls in his class that fall, and his feelings for Claire Ellen faded. The memory would flood Claire Ellen's mind each Spring when she smelled a profusion of lilacs.

After The Blizzard

Heather monitored the blizzard all weekend hoping that it would snow furiously causing school to be closed on Monday. The blizzard did not disappoint; it continued dumping snow over the area creating dazzling light and forming gigantic drifts and peaks of the brilliant white stuff. When the snow finally ceased falling late Sunday evening Heather found the world transformed, and when she woke on Monday morning it was a white paradise. The blizzard answered all prayers, and there was no school on Monday. As soon as Heather heard the news of the school closings on the radio she shouted with joy, and as she rejoiced the phone rang.

"Heather, Hi it's Charlie. How would you like to go sledding at Maple Trees Country Club's golf course? Bruce is calling Liz now to ask her."

"But, Charlie? Maple Trees is eons away, and we'd have to walk the whole way in this weather with the roads hardly plowed to capacity."

"Heather, it will be an adventure. Let's go. You won't believe the sledding. The hills at the golf course are so great you'll flip."

Charlie's pleas convinced Heather as his wishes had done during the last few months when they had been dating. When Liz telephoned, Heather learned that Bruce had fared as well with Liz. However, Heather's mother protested saying that the girls were not using good judgment and would most likely be sorry if they ventured out. She finally agreed to let Heather go warning her that she would be responsible for her own actions.

Liz lived two houses away from Heather so the boys picked them up almost simultaneously. The foursome met in front of Heather's house and started hiking toward the Country Club. The relentless wind whipped behind or in front of them and blew the snow up from the colossal mounds piled on either side of the walking path into their faces. It was like a whirlwind.

The endeavor proved awesome since it took almost an hour to walk the distance under good conditions. On this windy morning Heather gradually comprehended that this walk in the cold wind could last three or four hours. No one carried lunch along, and after taking a poll they realized that they didn't have enough money to buy lunch either. During the last hour of the walk when small talk petered out because of fatigue, Heather began to think the plan ridiculous.

But when the group reached the Country Club's golf course and Heather beheld the hills available for sledding all her apprehensions vanished. They carried their sleds up to the top of the highest hill, and Charlie taunted Heather into going first.

"Oh, Charlie. You don't have to tease me to get me to

do this. I can't wait," she said and flung herself belly first onto the sled. Exhilarated just by being there, Heather exhausted in the ride down. Her reddish brown hair flew wildly in all directions, her mittens got soaked, and the air froze her cheeks, but she took no notice of these minor matters. She thrilled to the swift descent. After she plummeted down the hill, the rest followed one by one with Charlie first and Liz last. Once down they shouldered their sleds and commenced climbing the hill again. For two hours they sledded tirelessly. Heather jolted herself back to reality when she finally glanced at her watch and realized that it was after 2 p.m.

"If we don't get going soon," she said, "it will be dark by the time we get home."

Reluctantly they headed away from the golf course toward Heather and Liz's part of town. The afternoon had turned even colder, and as experienced by King Wenceslas's page the wind was cruel. As they trudged home disagreeable things happened. Liz who had been dating Bruce mostly because Heather and her friends were dating the boys in Charlie's crowd and Bruce was his best friend displayed signs of irritation toward him. He was a shy, short boy with an unfortunate squeak in his voice who was at this time going through a bad time. His father, recently convicted for embezzlement, was now spending time in jail. The shock of this event caused Heather and her friends to treat Bruce with extreme care. Heather noticed that the current situation must have got to Liz, and she watched Liz relax her tactful treatment of him. Charlie seized this moment and flirted with Liz. Heather's jealousy caused her to feel animosity for the whole group.

Heather hatched a plan to pool the money they had on them and take a bus for at least the part of the trip that the bus covered. Once in the bus camaraderie didn't return, and things grew ugly. Heather nursed her jealousy and sneaked peeks at Charlie who increased his warmth toward Liz. In Heather's opinion, Liz reveled in Charlie's annoying attentions. Bruce seemed so hurt by this juncture that he said nothing to anyone during the entire bus ride. When the bus ride was over, Bruce lit out toward his home without a backward glance. Obviously, Heather thought, he isn't even planning to walk Liz home. Heather watched Charlie grow more expansive with Bruce's departure and more cavalier regarding Liz's welfare. By this time the three of them limped and felt wind burned and sick with exhaustion.

When they finally reached Heather's house their clothes soaked, she lit a fire and made hot chocolate and served cookies. Now Heather was miserable, and she watched in disbelief as Charlie plunked himself down on the couch in the middle of her and Liz and put his arms around both of them. She experienced a fury she didn't know she possessed. She would not share a boyfriend!

The next day neither Heather nor Liz went to school as both were too ill from exposure, but the joy Heather first felt after the blizzard disappeared. She always thought of the time after the blizzard as the time after Charlie. She and Charlie became just friends when Heather experienced seeing his arms around both her and Liz.

About The Author

Susan C. Barto was *born* on the beautiful day of June 21, 1941. The beloved child of Eda and Wiliam Forcellon. As she grew up she met a terrific man (Harry W. Barto) who later became her loving husband. Later Susan gave birth to a handsome baby boy (William M. Barto).

Susan's *educational* background was developed at Katherine Gibbs School and Union College, NJ. She has traveled extensively to Egypt, Italy, England and France.

She has experience with two years Legal Secretary - Legislative Aide; A writer for the last ten years. Her *memberships* include President Friends of the Hunterdon Museum of Art — New Providence Library Board, NJ — Raritan Valley College Book Group.

Susan Barto's *honors* are: Golden Certificate Award, Drury's Publishing™ — Plaque from Library Board, Listed in 1999-2000 Who's Who In The East and 2000 Who's Who In America, and Who's Who In Literary Achievement.

Her *publishing credits* include eleven stories published with Creative With Words, One story published with Yesterday's Magazette, One story published with Writer's Guidelines and News, One story published with Good Old Days, and several stories published with Drury's Publishing™, along with four books of stories published by Drury's Publishing™.

On a more *personal note* Susan C. Barto says: ***"I love to write. Writing defines who I am."***

www.ingramcontent.com/pod-product-compliance
Lightning Source LLC
Chambersburg PA
CBHW061524050726
47503CB00016B/2738